For the little monsters: Zoe, Kieran, Alexander, and Edward   M.R.

For Lidia   S.H.

Text by Mark Robinson
Illustrations copyright © 2010 Sarah Horne
This edition copyright © 2010 Lion Hudson

The moral rights of the author and illustrator
have been asserted

A Lion Children's Book
an imprint of
Lion Hudson plc
Wilkinson House, Jordan Hill Road, Oxford OX2 8DR
www.lionhudson.com
Paperback ISBN 978 0 7459 6167 5
Hardback ISBN 978 0 7459 6254 2

First UK edition 2010
1 3 5 7 9 10 8 6 4 2 0
First US edition 2010
1 3 5 7 9 10 8 6 4 2 0

A catalogue record for this book is available
from the British Library

Typeset in 17/22 Tempus Sans ITC
Printed in China May 2010 (manufacturer LH06)

Distributed by:
UK: Marston Book Services Ltd, PO Box 269, Abingdon, Oxon OX14 4YN
USA: Trafalgar Square Publishing, 814 N Franklin Street, Chicago, IL 60610

Then off outside to play some sports and be extremely mean, inflicting pain on *everyone*, not just the other team.

When school is done, the monsters all are keen to be away.
Just see how fast they shoot off home, for yet more work and play.